THE BLACKENED MIRROR

A Short Story

MADHU BAZAZ WANGU

Year of the Book
135 Glen Avenue
Glen Rock, PA 17327

This book is a work of fiction. Names, characters, places, and incidents are products of the author's imagination or are used fictitiously. Any resemblance to actual events or locations or persons, living or dead, is entirely coincidental.

ISBN: 978-1-64649-365-4 (paperback)
ISBN: 978-1-64649-366-1 (ebook)

OTHER BOOKS

Fiction

The Last Suttee

The Other Shore

The Immigrant Wife

Chance Meetings

Non-Fiction

Unblock Your Creative Flow

Images of Indian Goddesses

A Goddess is Born

Hinduism

Buddhism

CDs

Mindful Meditation for Writers: Body, Heart, Mind

Mindful Meditation for Writers II: Walking Through the Forest, Awakening the Senses, Mountain and Lotus, Animating Seven Energy Chakra

Meditations for Mindful Writers III: Generosity, Gratitude, Self-Compassion and Trust

I was a portrait painter. Young and self-taught, I started by copying black-and-white images of wrinkled old people, famished children, laborers carrying loads, and farmers plowing fields: all working for food and shelter. I knew their pain, their suffering. My mother was a bricklayer, and I, a dreamer. Each of us owned two sets of clothing. One covered our body and the other hung daily in the sun to dry. My mother worked hard for the builder to provide us with two meals a day, but I was content with only one if I could buy art supplies to depict moments in people's lives.

From the time I was nine until I turned sixteen, my aim was to feel at one with the person I painted. I also became conscious of my mother's struggle to survive. I sold my first work for a pittance. My mother tried persuading me to be a bricklayer, but she did not succeed. The day she discovered what I did while she was at the construction site, she hit me hard, so hard that I bled. From then on, I hid my work from her. It frustrated her that I idled away my days doing unpaid work.

"It is a sin to waste a life!" she screamed one day.

"I am not wasting my life. I do what no one else can do!" I said, then brought out artwork from underneath my bed and placed it before her.

One by one, she looked at each drawing until tears welled in her eyes. From that day on, she stopped pestering me. When she returned home every evening, she demanded to see my work. She looked, critiqued, and encouraged me to hone my skills and transform unfortunate people's lives into beautiful art. She began showing off my work to neighbors. Some expressed amazement at my God-given talent. A few disdained me for not being man enough to take care of my mother. I paid no heed; art consumed me.

One scorching hot afternoon, two men brought my mother's corpse home. Sunstroke had killed her. I was devastated. For months I neglected my art, and with it, myself. I suffered alone. Everyone suffers, but each of us suffers in his own way.

Around this time, I turned eighteen and decided to sell my art on the street. I spread a dhurrie on the busiest corner in my neighborhood. I sat on it, capturing the semblances of celebrities from their photographs—famous leaders, well-known personalities, Bollywood stars—and put them up for sale. My imitations drew people's attention. Passersby stopped for a few minutes to watch me draw and paint.

"That is so lifelike!" a man said.

"God has blessed you with such a gift, son!" an elderly lady commented.

"Can you draw my face? I'll give you twenty rupees!" a young man asked.

"Twenty rupees, sir? Twenty rupees for all that work?" I said and stared hard at him.

"How much do you want?"

"Fifty?"

"Are you a conman or an artist?" he said.

I ignored him and continued to draw.

"That line he just drew is worth twenty rupees!" someone shouted. "Give him what he is asking!"

"Why don't you get your picture made?" the first man said with irritation.

"If I had the money, I would!" the shouting man replied. "What about thirty rupees?"

"What about thirty-five?" I said, my heart beating fast.

That was my first. Soon after I raised my price to fifty, then seventy. Soon, people were paying a hundred rupees to get their faces drawn. I made hundreds of faces—profile or full face, bust or full-length, monochromatic or in color.

A year after selling my first portrait, I installed a canvas canopy to protect me from rain and heat. I set a wooden table and comfortable chair beneath it. On another table, I displayed several portraits of famous people. Passersby took notice.

One day, as I was absorbed in sketching a scene, I heard someone say, "*O ladke*! Hey boy, this is not the way for a fine artist to work—like a beggar!" I looked up. A well-dressed older man had picked up a portrait and was examining it.

"Not a beggar, sahib! I am a painter of portraits," I said with pride.

The man introduced himself as Ravi Verma. He said for the last thirty years he had painted billboards advertising the Bollywood movies showing in the local cinema halls. However, he no longer had the energy of a young man to paint large works by himself. He needed an assistant. He offered me my first job. I was only too happy to accept.

Ravi Verma took me to his studio, which looked more like a warehouse. I was awed at the size of the heads and torsos and hands he drew on forty-by-thirty-foot canvases. They looked monumental compared to the eight-by-eleven or twelve-by-twenty-inch surfaces I drew on. My works seemed miniscule in comparison, and I couldn't wait to paint gigantic portraits.

Ravi Verma asked me to call him Vermaji. For the first few days, I observed him painting. He drew a grid on the white gesso surface that I helped prepare. He stood on scaffolding facing the canvas and drew ovals, circles, triangles, and rectangles until a composition of a group of people came alive—all whom I readily recognized as famous Bollywood stars. I watched as he transformed the two-dimensional surface into a three-dimensional scene. He brought familiar faces to life on screen-size canvases: heroines with almond eyes, luscious lips, and voluptuous busts and hips; heroes with handsome faces and dreamy eyes. His depiction of lanky or stocky villains, all with lecherous expressions, smoking cigarettes or holding glasses of whiskey amused me.

For the first few months as an apprentice, I was given the work of stretching raw canvas on wooden frames, applying gesso on the surfaces, and mixing and blending colors. In time, he let me fill in large areas with the appropriate flat paint. That did not require much skill, but it helped me gain confidence in working on large areas. After a day's work, I washed brushes and bowls and cleaned the floor splashed with multi-colored paint.

Within one year under Vermaji's supervision, I had learned to shade a chignon or show a curl on a heroine's forehead. Slowly, I learned how to paint ears, hands, and eyes and make them look real. Finally, I painted a face without his assistance.

The best day of my life was when he let me paint all the figures on a billboard. Upon examining the completed work, he said, "The student has become the master."

I initially thought I had misunderstood, but from then on, he filled in the large surfaces with flat paint and I painted the figures and faces. I was ready for it. My skill and passion had been transformed into something much more than I had imagined. Full of energy, I painted with my whole body.

Relieved to see that someone would continue his legacy, one day Vermaji said, "Your work vibrates with emotions. Hear me, son. You will go places."

Eventually, I began to get bored with painting the same faces over and over again. The excitement of copying famous Bollywood stars from photographs was gone, and I wanted to paint live models and make portraits with personality. I wanted to work independent of restraints and make vibrant and original portraits. I grew restless to leave but did not want to disappoint the man who had supported me when I was nobody. I had developed an affection for my employer. Would he get angry? Would he be sad? When I opened my heart to him, though, Vermaji understood my frustrations and my desires. He said he too was thinking of closing the business, of retiring. I thanked him for being my mentor, and we bid each other a sad but friendly good-bye.

Like the Bollywood stars that I had painted for five years, I dreamed about becoming rich and famous. I did not want to work in a warehouse; I wanted to work in a studio, and have my own atelier. I did not want to live in an ordinary flat; I desired my own house. No, a mansion. I wanted to possess a motorbike. No, a car. I imagined a life of opulence and luxury.

Vermaji had given me the names and addresses of potential clients who were wealthy, and I introduced myself and showed them my portfolio. I looked covetously at their mansions and vehicles, and told myself, *All in good time, all in good time!*

Within days, I found my first patron, a director-producer with an unattractive face and manners but a very attractive purse. He was pleased with what I had done. No sooner had I finished that commission than my name spread wildly by word of mouth. I received so many jobs that I was kept occupied for a year. The more portraits I made, the more recognition I received. Although I exhibited my work in group shows, I had enough paintings for a solo exhibition. My patrons were glad to oblige me when I asked to borrow their portraits, especially when they learned that they would be displayed for other people to admire.

I first gained recognition at the local and state level, but then reviews of my shows began to appear in national newspapers. By the time I was in my late thirties, my deep driving desires had become reality. Art connoisseurs knew my name, and art admirers recognized my work. When the Ministry of Culture and Arts constructed an extension to their building, they asked me to paint four murals: Mahatma Gandhi, Rabindranath Tagore, Jawaharlal Nehru, and Indira Gandhi.

I painted the semblances of those great personalities, and I painted life-size images of city and suburban folks—suited and booted businessmen and local personalities looking smug as they posed, women decked in ornaments studded with gems modeling their silk and chiffon saris, and children dressed in fashionable clothes sitting restlessly to have their faces painted so as not to disappoint eager parents.

The more paintings I made, the more famous I became. All the families in society's upper echelon wanted my portraits to adorn the drawing rooms of their mansions. I received more commissions than I could handle. My savings account ballooned like a man who overeats. Was this the life I had wished for?

I met Shanti at the opening of one of my exhibitions. She was a writer and a lover of painting.

She had accompanied her father, a real estate magnate, to my show. Before they left, he asked if I would paint a portrait of him and his daughter, and I agreed

I arrived at their home with my painting paraphernalia. They had selected a room, a chair, and a pose in which to have their image made—the father in a Nehru jacket and churidaar pajama, seated in an elaborately carved walnut seat, and the daughter standing next to him in a silk and brocade sari, decked in her late mother's gem-studded gold ornaments. I couldn't take my eyes off her. They posed for hours, the father's expression lost in thoughts and the daughter smiling intently at me with her dark almond-shaped eyes. Her presence inspired me to make one of my best works. The day I signed my name to their portrait, I asked her if she would marry me. She consented.

We honeymooned in the valley of Kashmir, and returned there annually to holiday and celebrate our love. But gradually, our holiday time—I should say my holiday time—dwindled, and soon we stopped vacationing altogether. Why? Because I could not say no to new commissions. My work consumed me.

For the next few years, Shanti did not complain. She would spend a couple of weeks with her best friend Shakila, instead. More years flew by. By the fifth year, she begged me to take a break from work, something she would have never done earlier. She suggested we take a few days away from my so-called "creating." I did not stop to think what she meant nor pay heed to the fact that she wanted my attention. I was obsessed, more with myself than my art. Money was pouring in, and I didn't see any reason to block its flow.

Fortunately, though, I did not ignore the cues and clues my body had begun to give me. I heard it telling me to STOP and breathe in the life that was passing by so quickly. My back ached a bit, and at times my joints felt swollen and my legs more tired at the end of the day than previously. Yet I pushed these signals aside, still more concerned with how to delineate my clients' appearances with elegance and power than with paying attention to the message of an inner voice.

One fine spring evening, my wife and I were invited for dinner at the house of one of my old patrons, a businessman turned friend, Manoj Pathak. I had painted him, his wife, and their four children. The portraits hung in their living room and hallway. By now, painting silky black hair, black almond eyes, and beautiful skin had become second nature to me. I could paint a picture with my own eyes closed—their creative significance and their uniqueness superficial, confined to their surfaces, as deep as the color pigment.

After enjoying a sumptuous dinner, we sat on their back porch to have hot masala tea.

"Life seems to be going quite well for you, young man!" the elderly businessman said as he patted my back. "You have everything a man dreams of! Could you imagine all this when you painted the billboards?"

"I couldn't! I'm fortunate!" I said. "Yet life seems to be flying by, don't you think?" I don't know why I said this to Manoj.

"Indeed! But we can't hold on to life, can we?" he said thoughtfully. "Anyway, I have something to tell you that should please you."

"Good news is always welcome!" I was eager to hear what he had to say.

"Recently, I had a chance to meet the Maharaja of Saurashtra. He was searching for a portrait painter. I told him about you and your extraordinary skill. He wants to get his and the maharani's portrait made."

"Oh!" I should have been thrilled. But I was not. "Thanks for your recommendation, but Ashok Patel, a young artist, is as good," I muttered.

"Of course he is! But this commission is for you, my dear friend. This is the opportunity of a lifetime!" He sounded more enthusiastic than me. "And the honorarium will be something you could only dream of." He moved, crossing his legs.

To my own surprise, I did not want to travel. I asked, "Is the maharaja planning a long stay and a trip to New Delhi? It would take me several weeks to paint a double portrait."

"Oh no! No, no! He is not planning to travel. Too much responsibility in his state, you know!" he said, giggling with pleasure.

"How does he expect me to paint his picture?"

"You have to go to Saurashtra." He narrowed his eyes.

At that moment, our wives joined us. Our host repeated to Shanti the maharaja's desire to have a double portrait painted. She said something about her own portrait with her father, and said, "At least this patron will take him away from his studio."

While driving back home, I asked Shanti if she thought I had traded my creative freedom for popularity and wealth. At first she did not respond. When I repeated my question, she said my asking that question meant I partly believed it.

"I don't know, but something from within is bubbling up, putting a doubt in my mind about my art."

"I have been begging you to take a break, get away from it for a while. Perhaps this trip will do you good. You'll return refreshed and renewed. Perhaps you'll make something original."

"You think we should accept the maharaja's offer, then?" I looked expectantly at her.

"I don't know about the maharaja's offer, but going to Manipur Village in Saurashtra sounds like a good idea."

"How do you know about this village?" I was glad to hear her excitement about visiting this place.

"Shakila has a cabin there. It sounds like the most picturesque and mysterious town," she said. "There is magic in the air, she says. Your mind will clear, your heart open, and your anxieties dissipate. Trust me, I feel it," Shanti said with her hand on her heart. "Perhaps we can spend some days in Shakila's cabin before you see the maharaja!"

In a cabin? In some godforsaken village? "Why don't we stay in a hotel?"

"Not a hotel. You'll love this place. So inspiring! Shakila spends a few months there every summer. She is not going this summer, though."

Having ignored my dear wife's wishes for so long, I couldn't say no to her.

It had been a month since the evening at the businessman's house. We left my atelier and our mansion behind. We traveled by train to the unfamiliar and unknown village that Shakila found magical and which had mesmerized my wife.

From Ahmedabad, we took a bus toward Manipur. We drove on unpaved paths through cornfields where stalks were ready for harvesting. Enclosed in husks, ripe yellow corn lay hidden behind silky golden hair. We crossed chili fields lush with the long pointed green leaves of red-hot pepper plants. Our bus made one stop for passengers to use the latrines and step down to a historic well. Reaching into the water, we cupped our hands to drink and cool our parched throats, quench our thirst, and wash our faces.

Women in intricately embroidered backless cholis, blouses and brightly colored, heavily pleated, long skirts sold glass bangles and handmade trinkets. Their profiles were blurred behind muslin veils. In an open-air market, turbaned men, majestic in their white kurtas and pajamas, sold vegetables and fruit in circular baskets.

The bus dropped us at the edge of a vast field, and the only way to reach our destination was by bullock cart. We hired one, hopped in, and held our suitcases between our legs as the bullocks trotted off. The cart scurried along a rough path flanked by red pepper fields. Water-filled potholes splashed us, and the blue sky above blessed us.

At the edge of the pepper fields, the driver cried, "Ruk! Ruk!" and the bullocks halted. The driver asked us to jump out and stood to help us. I climbed out as he helped my wife down. With only a loincloth around his waist, I could see his ribs and shoulder blades. Exposed to the sun, the hue of his dark skin had intensified. I was reminded of childhood when my mother and I had little to eat, just struggling to keep our body and soul together. He was the kind of man I used to paint. I tipped him more than his week's salary. He said if I liked he would wait for me as long as I wanted. He would drive us whenever and wherever we wanted to go. I thanked him but gently refused his offer.

A boy stood watching as the driver left, then walked closer to us.

"Do you know a caretaker by the name of Jaidev?" I asked. He nodded.

"Where is he?"

Jaidev was to give us the key to Shakila's cabin. The boy nodded again and asked us to follow him. He led us away from the flaming expanse of pepper fields to a narrow lane before stopping in front of a mud hut. Then he disappeared as abruptly as he had appeared.

Shanti and I beheld the dramatic view of a solitary hut silhouetted under a large banyan tree. The rays of the setting sun haloed the dwelling. In the background, iridescent orange colored the western sky into a heavenly space. From where we stood, details were blurred, but a swing hanging on the front porch became visible. A circular window behind the swing mesmerized me, inviting me in. I felt an urge to enter the hut. We walked toward the porch and ascended five steps.

Shanti, tired from the day's journey, settled on the swing to rest. I peered through the circular window and saw the interior of an unfurnished room, which I entered through the door. No smell. No color. Inside, on the front wall, I saw a blackened mirror hanging on a nail beneath an alcove. I picked it up. There was no reflection. Its black surface stared back at me. Then something uncanny happened. I felt uneasy, alone. I do not know why. I felt as if I had lost something. No, I had an urge to search for something, but did not know what I was supposed to find. Suddenly I felt as though I would amount to nothing until I found this nameless object.

I wanted to walk out and sit next to my wife. When I turned to leave, I saw an old man sitting in the corner of the room, behind the open door. Seated on a mat, he sat with his legs crossed. His hair was matted, his eyes half-closed. He had a beige shawl wrapped around his upper body. His left hand was placed over his left knee, the thumb touching his index finger. With his right hand, he was turning a rosary. Who was he? Jaidev's father?

"Namaskar, Babaji!" I greeted him. My voice croaked. I cleared my throat. Sitting still, he continued to turn the string of beads.

Feeling like an intruder, I did not want to disturb him more than I had.

The bitter smell of burnt rice drew me toward the kitchen. A pot of rice on the mud hearth had boiled over; it was dried and charred. The coal had turned to ash, and smoke seemed to escape through the window above the hearth. It left a lingering odor. The sunlight reflected upon the still life, and I paused. Making a viewfinder by crossing two fingers of my two hands and looking through it, I slowly pivoted on my heels with knees gently bent. I stopped at different positions when my finger-frame focused on an appealing view. Compositions of white, black, gray, and orange gold surfaced in my consciousness. The evening light glistened on the pots and pans as it brushed their surfaces; the sheen of highlights contrasted with dark kitchen nooks. My creative instincts gushed. How I wished I had my canvas and paints! But the burnt odor drew me back to the present.

I stepped from the kitchen to the porch. In the silence I heard water dripping from a faucet at the other end of the hut where Shanti rested. Seeing her eyes closed, I tiptoed toward the drip. The water had filled a tin bucket that now overflowed. I tightened the faucet and returned to sit on the swing at the small space left near my wife's feet. The swing creaked and woke her.

"Did you get the keys?" she asked with her eyes closed.

"Not yet." I could not wipe the image of the blackened mirror from my mind.

"Didn't you find the caretaker?" She raised her head, her eyes half-closed.

"I will. Shanti, I feel something in this house... something I cannot describe... something..."

"What are you talking about?" She sat up.

"I found a blackened mirror that I can't get out of my mind. A man is meditating in that room. Something in there is calling me back. Stay here until I return."

I walked back inside. The old man's eyes were still closed. I strode to the alcove and picked up the mirror. I needed to see my face, but it wasn't there. What could this be? Black paint? Soot? I pulled my monogrammed white handkerchief from my pocket and used spit to rub the surface of the mirror, first mildly, then frantically. Slowly, the gunk and grime came off. I walked to the water faucet, wet the soiled handkerchief, and again rubbed the surface until it glistened. In the process of cleaning the mirror, the handkerchief turned into a dirty rag.

I walked back to the room with the mirror in hand. From the window I saw Shanti pacing outside the hut. I looked at my reflection. It looked back at me, piercing me with its gaze. *Who are you?* A soundless voice startled me. It was as if I were looking at myself for the first time. At that moment, someone's presence startled me.

"It scared you, didn't it?" Babaji stood in front of me.

"What did?" I asked, aghast.

"The dark mirror!" Babaji smiled. "I too was unable to see my true reflection—inward. I must have been your age then... it was years ago... when I saw my Self."

"Why is it that since I found this mirror I have felt confused, disintegrated?" I was desperate to know, and Babaji asked me to sit down. We sat cross-legged on the floor facing each other. He asked me about myself, and I gave him the highlights of my life while he listened attentively.

"As a child, dear son, you were your authentic Self. But as you grew older, your desire for power, possessions, and position increased. You showed only your masked face to the world, even to your Self. So much so that you began to see your Self as others saw you—with a mask. Your authentic Self, thus neglected, went dormant."

"I don't remember losing touch. When did I put on the mask?" I asked.

"When you became disconnected from your heart. When you started to paint only semblances of people. When instead of expressing your deep-seated urge to paint the human condition, you started to decorate surfaces. You got disconnected from your heart, your soul. This is your story, my story, the story of everyone, whether you are professionally successful or unsuccessful, rich or poor. Ultimately, each one of us at some point in our lives must face the emptiness of our masked Selves and search for our authentic Self."

Babaji continued. "Many years ago, I tried to look at my own reflection. Hidden behind it, I saw someone else. Who was it whose heart beat in unison with mine? Was someone else beside me living within, equally engaged in my daily affairs? But I did not pay attention. Who was it that wore the clothes I wore, lived in my house, witnessed my thoughts, actions, words, watched over me, and when I was at a crossroads, nudged me in the right direction? But I paid no heed; worldly affairs devoured me. I was enticed by pretense while my divine Self loved me from within."

At that moment, I felt charged with the same flow that used to pass through me when I was inspired. Long ago, it had directed me, taken pleasure in my work, and been my constant companion. Now I was controlled by outer circumstances. I was told what to do and when to do it. The quicksand of success had made me forget who I really was. I had let the dazzle of fame eclipse the light of my inspiration, the light of my life.

From the window, I saw Shanti attentively listening to a man. Before hanging the mirror back on the wall, I turned to thank Babaji, but he was gone. I stood alone in the room. His sudden disappearance jolted me. But I grounded myself and hung the mirror where I had found it, then walked back slowly to my wife.

"This is Jaidev, the caretaker," Shanti said.

"Sorry for the inconvenience, sir! Someone directed you to an abandoned house. Please follow me to my office. I'll hand you the keys to your cabin."

"Abandoned?"

"Yes, sir. Nobody has lived here in years. Some people even believe it is haunted. Please come."

I held Shanti's warm hand and squeezed it gently. She smiled back at me. We quietly followed Jaidev. As I stopped momentarily to take another look at the house, my earlier life reeled through my mind.

ABOUT THE AUTHOR

The founder of Mindful Writers Groups and Retreats, DR. MADHU BAZAZ WANGU has won awards from Writer's Digest, Feather Quill, Readers Favorite, Next Generation Indie Book, Indie Excellence, and TAZ Awards. She inspires novice as well as advanced creative people to become better writers and creators, and authentic human beings by following the practice of Writing Meditation.

Madhu has written about her own struggle, trials and tribulations as well as pleasurable experiences that have come her way and taught her what it means to feel awe, wonder and afterglow of creative flow. Currently she is writing her tenth book, the fifth fiction, tentatively titled, *Meaning of My Life*.

Dr. Wangu is a regular workshop presenter at writing conferences. She was the Featured Author at Beaver County Book Fest in 2017, Inaugural Guest at International Indo-American Literary Festival, 2020, and that year she won the Pennwriters Meritorious Award. She was the Lunch Keynote Speaker at Pennwriters Annual Conference in 2023.

Visit the website:
MadhuBazazWangu.com

OTHER BOOKS

Fiction

The Last Suttee

The Other Shore

The Immigrant Wife

Chance Meetings

Non-Fiction

Unblock Your Creative Flow

Images of Indian Goddesses

A Goddess is Born

Hinduism

Buddhism

CDs

Mindful Meditation for Writers: Body, Heart, Mind

Mindful Meditation for Writers II: Walking Through the Forest, Awakening the Senses, Mountain and Lotus, Animating Seven Energy Chakra

Meditations for Mindful Writers III: Generosity, Gratitude, Self-Compassion and Trust

9 781646 493654